LITTLE WOMEN

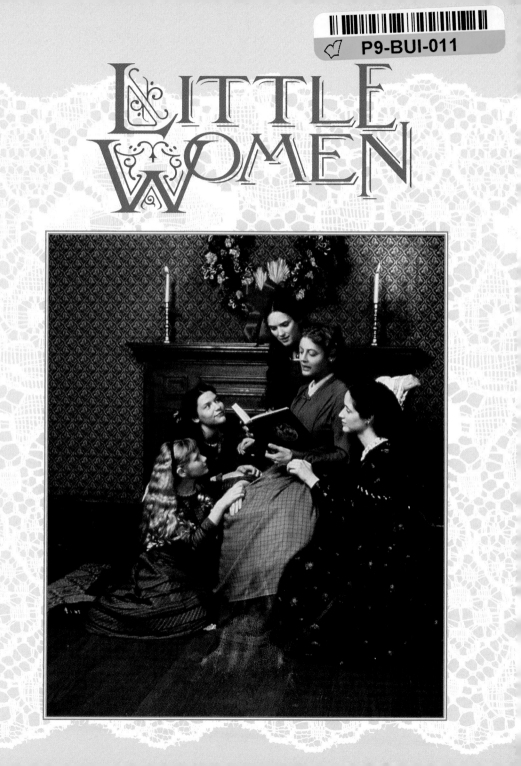

LITTLE WOMEN

Adapted by M. J. Carr
From the screenplay by Robin Swicord
Based on the novel by Louisa May Alcott

SCHOLASTIC INC.
New York Toronto London Auckland Sydney

COLUMBIA PICTURES PRESENTS
A DI NOVI PICTURES PRODUCTION A FILM BY GILLIAN ARMSTRONG WINONA RYDER "LITTLE WOMEN" GABRIEL BYRNE
TRINI ALVARADO SAMANTHA MATHIS KIRSTEN DUNST CLAIRE DANES CHRISTIAN BALE ERIC STOLTZ MARY WICKES AND SUSAN SARANDON
CO-PRODUCER ROBIN SWICORD SCREENPLAY BY ROBIN SWICORD PRODUCED BY DENISE DI NOVI DIRECTED BY GILLIAN ARMSTRONG   COLUMBIA PICTURES

ISBN 0-590-22538-3

Designed by Elizabeth B. Parisi

12 11 10 9 8 7 6 5 4 3 2 1   5 6 7 8 9/9 0/0

Printed in the U.S.A.   37

First Scholastic printing, January 1995

On the edge of a small New England town stood a cheerful clapboard house. In it lived the March family, who had four lively girls. Meg, Jo, Beth, and Amy were as different as sisters could be. Meg, the oldest, was graceful and demure. Jo was smart and full of spirit, as wild and fun as her unruly tousle of chestnut brown hair. Shy little Beth was sweet and kind. All those who knew her loved her. And Amy, the youngest, was a pretty young thing with a merry cap of golden curls.

One snowy Christmas Eve, the sisters gathered in the warm light of the upstairs garret. The girls had dressed up as boys and were having a meeting of their secret society. Jo tramped about in heavy boots. She had written an adventure story and was reciting it to her sisters.

The girls looked out the garret window at the large estate house that stood next to theirs. A coach had pulled up and a boy had arrived. It was Laurie, the grandson of old Mr. Laurence who lived there. The March girls were poor, but their neighbors were rich. Meg sighed.

"I wish we could have presents this year," she said.

"I wish the war was over," Beth added wistfully. "So Father could come home."

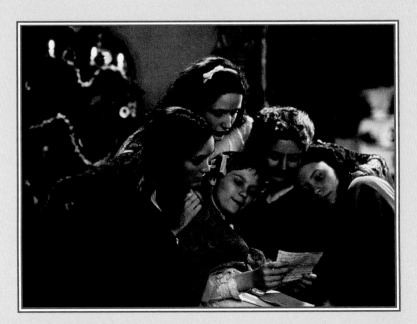

Downstairs, a door opened. Their mother had returned from work. "Marmee!" they cried. The girls clambered down the stairs in a bunch to greet her. One took her cape, another brushed the snow from her hair. In Marmee's pocket was a letter from their father. The girls crowded around as their mother read the letter, the best Christmas present of all.

The next morning, the girls were touched by the Christmas spirit. They bundled up the tasty breakfast that was to be their Christmas treat. Together, they marched off to bring the sweet sausages and buttered buns to a poor German family that lived down the way. On the road, they passed Mr. Laurence and Laurie. Jo waved the coffeepot in her blunt way.

"Lovely weather for a picnic!" she called out, joking.

Mr. Laurence winced. He nudged Laurie into their carriage.

Soon it was New Year's Day. Meg and Jo were invited to a grand party. They scrambled about, crimping their hair and ironing their frocks. Jo's dress was scorched in back, where she had stood too close to the fire. Meg shook her head at her sister's boyish ways. "You'll have to keep your back to the wall," she instructed.

At the party, Jo met Laurie. While others danced, Laurie and Jo romped harum-scarum through the corridor. This boy's not a snob! Jo thought with glee. He's a capital fellow!

When the party was over, Laurie offered the sisters a ride home in his carriage. Amy was waiting for them, watching from the stairs.

"Was he romantic?" she asked swooningly.

Jo laughed at her silly young sister. "I think he'll be our friend," she said.

When the holidays were over, Meg and Jo returned to work, and Amy to her school. The girls trudged through the wet, sloppy snow.

"Blast these wretched skirts!" cursed Jo.

"Why do I have to go to school?" complained Amy. "I don't even have any limes."

"Limes?" Jo snorted.

"They're all the fashion at school. My friends have given me ever so many."

Meg slipped Amy a quarter for limes.

"Jehoshaphat!" muttered Jo.

Jo trundled on to her job. She had to care for her crotchety old aunt. She knew Aunt March would harp and complain, as she always did.

"Josephine, read louder!"

"Josephine, there's a draft!"

Aunt March's pesky little poodle would yip and yap. Jo wished she could be back in the garret, writing her stories.

The days wore on. Jo kept busy and worked hard at her writing. The neighbor boy, Laurie, did indeed become her friend. He built a mailbox out of a birdhouse. He stuck it on the hedge that separated their houses. One day, Laurie left theatre tickets inside, one for Jo and another for Meg. Amy begged to go along, too.

"No." Jo was firm.

Amy pouted. "You'll be sorry, Jo March," she threatened.

When Jo came home, she clapped on her writing cap and hunted for the copybook in which she wrote her stories.

"Where's my manuscript?" she asked.

Amy smiled wickedly. Jo ran to the small wood stove that warmed the room. A fire was burning brightly. Her book! Amy had tossed it in the fire!

Jo grabbed ahold of Amy and shook her hard. "I hate you!" she swore. "I'll never forgive you! As long as I live!"

The next day, Jo and Laurie went ice skating at the pond. Amy was sorry that she had burned Jo's book. She chased after Jo, but Jo skated ahead. Amy ran onto a weak patch of ice. It cracked and gave way. Amy fell through!

"Amy!" shouted Jo.

Laurie fished the scared little girl out of the icy water. He and Jo bundled Amy up and hurried her home.

As Amy warmed herself before the fire, Jo started a new copybook. Amy peered over her sister's shoulder. "Don't forget the part about the duke," she offered in apology.

Jo smiled and put her arm around Amy. Together, the two sisters tried to remember the stories that had been burned. Together, they worked at writing them back down.

That spring, Meg was invited to a party in Boston. She packed her dresses. They were plain and shabby. The other girls at the party had frilly dresses made of silk. One of the girls took pity on Meg and lent her an elegant silk gown. Meg stepped into the party with her pretty shoulders bared. Her face was made up and her arms looped with bangles. It felt fun to look so stylish.

In the ballroom, Meg saw Laurie. They stepped into a quiet alcove to talk. There, they overheard two women gossiping about Meg.

"Did you see that March girl?" said one.

"She's got herself all dressed up, trying to catch that rich Laurence boy," scoffed the other.

Meg's face burned with shame. How could they think such a thing! When Meg returned home, Marmee consoled her. "People love to wag their tongues," she said. "Nonetheless, I hope that my daughters will always step out into the world with purpose and confidence."

Soon it was time for Laurie to pack up for college. Jo wished she could go, too. As Laurie sorted through his things, he told Jo a secret. John Brooke, his tutor, had fallen in love with Meg.

Jo was not pleased at the news. "Blast Mr. Brooke!" she cursed. She didn't want her sister to fall in love and get married. She wanted the sisters to stay together always.

That afternoon, a telegram arrived. Their father had been wounded in the war. Mrs. March would have to leave immediately for the hospital. The family had no money, though, to buy a ticket for the train.

Jo dashed out of the house. When she returned, she waved a roll of bills she clutched tightly in her fist. It was twenty-five dollars!

"How did you get the money?" her sisters asked.

Jo pulled off her hat. Her long, wild hair was now cropped short.

"I sold my hair," she said, grinning.

Mrs. March hugged her daughters and bid them good-bye. "I shall miss my little women," she said.

While their mother was gone, the girls tended the household themselves. Sweet little Beth took food to the German family that the girls had visited the Christmas before. When Beth arrived, the baby was sick. She picked it up and cradled it. She rocked it and cooed. But the baby still fussed and cried.

That night, when Beth got home, she fell ill as well. The baby had had scarlet fever. Now Beth had caught it, too.

Jo and her sisters nursed Beth with care. Still, Beth tossed and thrashed with fever. She grew weak and ghostly pale. The girls were frightened. They sent for their mother. It looked as if Beth might die.

At last, the fever broke. Beth began to grow stronger. She would never again, though, be as hardy as she had been before.

That Christmas, the March girls decked the house gaily with greenery. Mr. Laurence sent Beth a piano as a gift. There was much to celebrate. Their Beth was still alive.

As Beth sat down to play the piano, the family got another present. Mr. March walked in the door. He was bandaged and weary, but home from the war! Jo hugged her father joyfully and helped him with his boots. She took the boots outside to brush off the mud. There, she came upon Meg and John Brooke. They were in the doorway, kissing.

Changes were happening quickly at the March house. Too quickly for Jo.

Meg and John were soon married. Meg wore a simple white dress. At the wedding, Laurie linked his arm in Jo's and winked at her. Laurie had another secret, a secret of his own.

One day, as Jo was romping in the woods, Laurie slipped up behind her. Jo leaned against an old wood fence. Laurie had a confession to make. "Jo," he said carefully, "I'm in love with you, you know." He touched her hair tenderly. He leaned close to kiss her.

"Wait!" Jo cried.

"You don't love me?" Laurie asked.

"Of course I do. You're my dearest friend." Jo didn't want to hurt his feelings, but she had to tell the truth. "I love you as I would love a brother."

Laurie felt stung. He fled to his house. He locked himself in the parlor and played the piano long into the night. The sad songs drifted across the yard and into Jo's window. She hoped that Laurie would somehow forget her. She decided she must go away.

While Jo had been busy, Aunt March had taken another niece, young Amy, as her favorite. She decided to take Amy with her on a long trip to Europe. Jo was disappointed. She had hoped that she would be the one chosen to go to Europe with Aunt March. Jo packed up her things and headed to New York. There, she got a job as a governess. She worked on her stories whenever she could.

In the boardinghouse where Jo stayed, she was befriended by a German man who was a teacher. His eyes twinkled and his manner was kind. His name was Professor Bhaer.

Professor Bhaer guessed that Jo was a writer. Each week, she slipped off to take her stories to the offices of the publishing houses. She hoped that someone would publish her stories soon.

One day, Jo bounded up the steps of the boardinghouse. A newspaper had printed one of her stories! She held the paper out proudly to show Professor Bhaer. He squinted at the page.

"Your story is about vampires?" he asked, surprised. Professor Bhaer thought that Jo had better, more heartfelt stories to tell.

Jo's feelings were bruised. She had hoped Professor Bhaer would congratulate her. That night, to make up with her, he invited Jo to the opera.

Jo had never seen an opera before. She and Professor Bhaer sat on a catwalk above the stage. After the show, they wandered home through the snowy city streets. That night, New York seemed almost magical. "The snowflakes look like falling stars," said Jo.

Professor Bhaer leaned over and kissed her. Jo caught her breath. His kiss was tender, thrilling. It seemed that Jo had fallen in love.

Far away, across the ocean, Amy was traveling in France. There, the weather was warm and balmy. One day, as Amy stopped to sketch the lush, green landscape, she spotted Laurie. He had come to France to nurse his broken heart.

Laurie studied Amy. She'd bloomed and grown beautiful in the time she'd been away. Laurie was surprised at his feelings for her. Perhaps he could love someone else besides Jo after all.

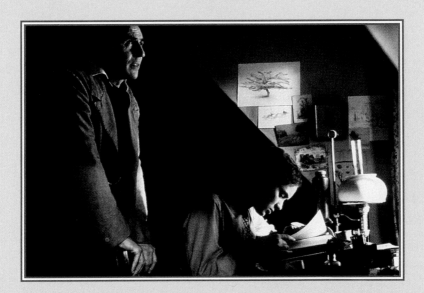

In New York, Jo worked hard on the novel she was writing. She had worked up a thrilling story filled with counts and daggers, pirates and sabers. She showed it to Professor Bhaer.

"Tell me what you think," she urged.

"I think you should write something more like life," he suggested, "something that is truer, from the depths of your soul. I think you have the courage to do so."

Once again, he'd hurt her feelings. Jo stalked off in a huff. When she reached her room, she flung her manuscript against the wall. Then she saw a telegram poking out under the door. It was from her mother. Beth had taken ill again. The telegram said she might die! Jo threw her things into her bag. She hurried home at once.

Jo was startled when she saw how sick her sweet sister had become. Beth had lost much weight. Her cheeks were hollow, her limbs thin.

"I'm glad you're home," Beth whispered.

Jo's eyes welled with tears.

"Don't worry," Beth said hoarsely. "I'm not afraid. But I know that I shall be homesick for you, even in heaven."

Jo clasped Beth's thin little hand.

"I won't let you go," she vowed.

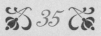

That night, when the moon ducked behind the clouds and the branches of the trees waved in the wind, Beth passed on. Jo took her sister's hand. It was light and lifeless. "Beth!" she wailed. "Oh, Beth!"

The March family cried. They buried their dear kind Beth. Her sweet little presence would no longer brighten their home.

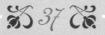

After Beth died, Jo wandered the woods in grief. She felt so alone. She missed her friend Laurie. She sent a letter to London where he had gone to work. In the letter, she told him about Beth. "Please, Laurie," she wrote, "will you come home to comfort me?"

But Laurie did not go to Jo. He thought, instead, of Amy, who was still in Europe, all alone. She would need comfort, too. Laurie realized that he had grown to love Amy. He traveled to the Alps to be at her side.

Because Jo was lonely, she took to writing in the garret, as she had when she was younger. This time, she didn't write farfetched stories about counts and daggers. This time, she wrote simply, as Professor Bhaer had suggested.

The stories Jo worked on were about her family. She wrote about the fun she and her sisters had had at Christmas, about the way Meg had dressed up for the ball. She wrote about Beth and her piano. About Amy and her limes. In that way, Jo kept her sisters with her. In that way, even Beth was still alive.

When Jo finished, she tucked the manuscript into a large envelope. She mailed it off to Professor Bhaer.

Time passed. Meg and John Brooke started a family. When Meg gave birth, it was to twins. One was a girl and the other a boy. Jo looked after her little niece and nephew. She heard not a word from Professor Bhaer.

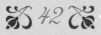

One crisp fall day, the front bell rang. It was Laurie. He had come home.

"May I present my wife," he said proudly. He pointed, behind him, to Amy.

Laurie? Married to Amy? Jo was stunned. The March family crowded around the two beaming newlyweds. Jo was happy for them. Still, she wished she had found someone who would love her, as her sisters had.

Soon after Laurie and Amy returned, Aunt March died. In her will, she left her large, rambling estate to Jo.

Mrs. March looked around the huge, old house. It was too big for Jo. "It would make a wonderful school," she suggested.

"A school..." Jo considered. It was a good idea. Jo knew, though, that she couldn't manage a school by herself.

With the spring came the rains. The warm rain softened the hard winter ground. One drizzly day, Jo found a large envelope on the kitchen table. It was her manuscript. It had been set in type by a publisher. Someone had bought it! It would soon be a book!

"A foreign gentleman left it," explained Hannah, the housekeeper.

It must be Professor Bhaer! Jo burst from the house to catch him. He was already on the road to the train.

Professor Bhaer stood wet and bedraggled in the light spring rain. Jo threw her arms around him.

"Thank you for my book," she cried.

Professor Bhaer smiled. He had arranged the whole surprise for her himself.

"I must be going," he said shyly. Professor Bhaer had missed Jo terribly, but didn't want to say so. He didn't think Jo cared for him. The last time he had seen her, they had quarreled. "Tomorrow I travel west to find a job teaching in

a school," he said. He looked away. He dug his toe in the mud.

Jo swallowed hard. If he left now, she would never see him again.

"I'm thinking of starting a school," she said quickly. "I'll need someone to teach. Would you stay here?"

Professor Bhaer turned and looked at her.

"Please stay with me," she pleaded tenderly. "Please don't go away."

Professor Bhaer grinned. His fondest wish was true! Jo March loved Friedrich Bhaer! Life would be sweet, after all.

As the rain splashed the trees and pattered on the mud, Professor Bhaer took Jo in his arms. Beneath the shelter of his ragged, worn umbrella, he kissed her. Jo smiled and took his hand. She led him back to her family's warm, cheerful house. The two sloshed home through the mud. Together, they would make a school. Together, they would share a good marriage and a long, happy life.